You're Somebody Special, Walliwigs!

For Niki Daly -
the inspirational force
behind Walliwigs

Also by Joan Rankin:
The Little Cat and the Greedy Old Woman
Scaredy Cat
Wow! It's Great Being a Duck

1 3 5 7 9 10 8 6 4 2

Copyright © Joan Rankin 1999

Joan Rankin has asserted her right under the
Copyright, Designs and Patents Act, 1988,
to be identified as the author and illustrator of this work

First published in the United Kingdom in 1999
by The Bodley Head Children's Books
Random House, 20 Vauxhall Bridge Road, London SW1V 2SA
by arrangement with The Inkman, Cape Town

Random House Australia (Pty) Limited, 20 Alfred Street, Milsons Point, Sydney
New South Wales 2061, Australia

Random House New Zealand Limited, 18 Poland Road, Glenfield
Auckland 10, New Zealand

Random House South Africa (Pty) Limited, Endulini, 5A Jubilee Road,
Parktown 2193, South Africa

Random House UK Limited Reg. No. 954009

A CIP catalogue record for this book
is available from the British Library

ISBN 0 370 32318 1

Printed in Singapore

You're Somebody Special, WALLIWIGS!

Joan Rankin

THE BODLEY HEAD
LONDON

Walliwigs' mother was a scatty parrot.
She made her nest in a very silly place.

One morning, during a little fly about over the
Botanical Gardens, the ship started to move.
It sailed out of the harbour.
Walliwigs could see the sea.
It was a blue and very big sea.

Walliwigs missed his lunch.
By supper time he was ravenous.
"Ma, I want my supper," he squawked.

The ship's cook looked out to see what all the fuss was about.

The Captain came out on the bridge and said,
"Call Sid the ship's boy to get that thing out
of my chimney!"

Sid, the ship's boy, loved climbing up chimneys, so that was okay.

He also loved his python, Harold.

You're so small and such a BIG nuisance.

But he did not love parrots.

When the ship arrived at the next port, Sid put
Walliwigs in a pineapple box and took him
ashore to his Aunty Beth.

Oh Sidney, what have you brought me this time?

Pineapple-Parrot Pie!
That doesn't sound
very nice.

When Sid had gone, Aunty Beth wondered
what to do with Walliwigs.

The only birds Aunty Beth liked were
her chickens. So she put Walliwigs
with one of her hens, Martha, and
hoped for the best.

"What is this?" said Martha,
inspecting the new arrival.

When she saw what it was, she clucked,

A Chick! A Chick!

The hens gathered round to inspect Martha's first child.
"He's very scrawny," said the ginger hen.
"He's very ugly," said the speckled hens.
But Martha didn't give a hoot.
She thought Walliwigs was gorgeous.

Martha spent all her time looking after him.
And Walliwigs thought that Martha was the
loveliest mum in the whole wide world. She
never let him out of her sight.

"That kid is not only scrawny and squawky, he also eats too much," said the ginger hen to the other hens.

"Nonsense," said Martha. "My Walliwigs has a wonderful appetite."

Walliwigs certainly
loved his food.

He ate all his supper,

and every day he grew **bigger,**

and bigger,

until Martha's nest
was too small.

Martha taught Walliwigs to roost beside her on the perch.

The real problem was – the more Walliwigs grew,
the less he looked like a chicken.
"Just look at those flat feet and silly feathers!"
gossiped the speckled hens.
"He's a misfit," said the ginger hen.
"He's not a misfit!" protested Martha.
"He's very special."

But it's not easy being different.

Flat feet! Silly feathers!

Soon Walliwigs began to feel lonely.

Then one afternoon, Professor Beak, an ornithologist who lived next door, said to Aunty Beth,
"Do you mind if I take a look at that bird that makes such an extraordinary sound in your backyard?"
When the professor saw Walliwigs, he exclaimed, "How remarkable! I must have it!"
"Help yourself," said Aunty Beth, who had had enough of Walliwigs' funny ways.
But Walliwigs wasn't at all keen to leave his mum.

Finally, Professor Beak shut Walliwigs in a special box for carrying birds to the Institute of Ornithology.

Walliwigs could be heard squawking and making a fuss all the way to the professor's car.

Martha was heartbroken. Martha was inconsolable.

Two weeks later a letter from the Institute of
Ornithology arrived for Martha. Aunty Beth read it
in front of everyone.

My darling Ma.

I am having a lovely time!
the Proffessor says that I am a
Proborciger aterimus. Thats a
special name for a Great Black
cockatoo. I am an endangered speaes
and I get special treatment.
I will be getting married as soon
as a suitable bride is found.
I love you
Walliwigs

Martha was overjoyed. She turned to the ginger hen and the speckled hens and said proudly, "There you are! I told you my Walliwigs was very special."

"Oh, Martha," said the ginger hen, "we would be very honoured if you would come up and sleep on our perch."

"Yes, yes, do please join us," clucked the speckled hens....

... but Martha was much too busy planning something smashing to wear for the wedding.